SONG LEE AND THE "I HATE YOU" NOTES

OTHER BOOKS BY SUZY KLINE

SONG LEE AND
THE "I HATE YOU" NOTES

BY SUZY KLINE
Pictures by Frank Remkiewicz

Viking

VIKING

Published by the Penguin Group

Penguin Putnam Books for Young Readers,

345 Hudson Street, New York, New York 10014, U.S.A.

Penguin Books Ltd, 27 Wrights Lane, London W8 5TZ, England

Penguin Books Australia Ltd, Ringwood, Victoria, Australia

Penguin Books Canada Ltd, 10 Alcorn Avenue, Toronto, Ontario, Canada M4V 3B2

Penguin Books (N.Z.) Ltd, 182-190 Wairau Road, Auckland 10, New Zealand

Penguin Books Ltd, Registered Offices: Harmondsworth, Middlesex, England

First published in 1999 by Viking,

a member of Penguin Putnam Books for Young Readers.

1 3 5 7 9 10 8 6 4 2

LIBRARY OF CONGRESS CATALOGING-IN-PUBLICATION DATA

Kline, Suzy.

Song Lee and the "I hate you" notes /

by Suzy Kline : pictures by Frank Remkiewicz.   p.   cm.

Summary: Song Lee is upset when she receives hateful notes in

class, but she finds an appropriate and positive way to deal with them.

ISBN 0-670-87887-1 (hc.)

[1. Schools—Fiction. 2. Behavior—Fiction. 3. Korean Americans—

Fiction.] I. Remkiewicz, Frank, ill. II. Title.

PZ7.K6797Sn 1999 [Fic]—dc21 98-41376 CIP AC

Printed in U.S.A.

Set in Century Schoolbook

Acknowledgments:

Special appreciation to my editor, Cathy Hennessy,
for her valuable help with this manuscript,
to Bernard Waber for his classic book, *Lovable Lyle,*
to Beverly Cleary for her classic, *Ramona the Pest,*
and to my husband for his helpful comments.

For My Class, with Love

Mario Allison
Cassandra Anderson
Danielle BeBault
David Bechard
Anthony Biancardi
Keith Carlson
Nicholas Corbo
Peter Damis
Barrett Donna
Thomas Filippini
Forrest Ford
Carly Greco
Evan Hill
Alison Jarvis
Heath Jenkins
Jessica Kiback
Brian LaTulipe
Alexandre Lent
Carissa Plante
Samantha Pratt
Kelly Richnavsky
Brittany Rocheleau
Melissa Roscello
Tyler Ruby
Julianne Toce
Jared Todd
Patricia Weingart
Erik Wilcox

Contents

SONG LEE AND
THE "I HATE YOU" NOTES

Flies and Other Pests

I never thought I would tell this story.

Not in a million years.

My name is Doug. I write about my class. Most stories are about Harry. He's my best friend who loves to do horrible things.

Sometimes I write about Song Lee. She's the nicest person in our class. Everyone likes her. I never thought *Song Lee* would ever do something horrible.

But that's what this story is about.

It all began on a gray October day in third grade. We were sitting on the rug in the library corner for morning conversation. Dexter had just finished talking about his new septic tank. "We can flush our toilet now," he said.

Song Lee giggled.

When Miss Mackle called on Sidney, he stopped chewing his gum. "You know my new last name, La Fleur, is French. Well, now my stepdad is teaching me French. Last night I learned *fair may la boosh*. That means 'be quiet.'"

"Very good, Sidney," Miss Mackle replied. "You'll have to share more French words with us, but *first* you need to spit out that wad of gum."

Sidney made a face as he walked

over to the wastepaper basket and spit it out. The gum went *thunk* when it hit the bottom of the can.

Mary continued our conversation. "This is a picture of our new black lab. Mom and Dad are taking him to puppy school."

"How interesting," Miss Mackle replied. "Is that where they learn commands?"

"Yes. So far Newton knows *sit* and *lie down*."

"Did you name him after the cookie, Fig Newton?" Ida asked.

Mary peered over her glasses. "No," she snapped. "We named him after the scientist, Sir Isaac Newton."

"I wish I could go to puppy school," Harry interrupted.

Mary groaned, "Me too. But . . . my parents won't let me go with them because . . ."

The class waited for her to finish a yawn.

". . . it's an evening class and past my bedtime. It's not fair. I never get a chance to do anything."

"*Say doe mazj,*" Sidney replied. "That means 'too bad' in French."

"Thank you Sidney, and Mary," Miss

Mackle replied. "Now, Song Lee, what did you have to share?"

"A jar of dead flies. I got them from our windowsill. I thought our African water frog might like them."

"Neat-o!" Harry said. He and Song Lee love to collect bugs.

Dexter ran his fingers through his new third-grade hairdo. That was his Elvis way of saying "cool."

"May I see one of those flies?" Miss Mackle asked.

Song Lee unscrewed the jar and shook one into the palm of her hand. "Sure."

Miss Mackle got up and went over to the microscope. She put the fly on a little rectangular piece of glass. "Want to take a closer look?" she said adjusting a knob. "There, it's focused."

"Ooooooooooh," Song Lee cooed. "What a beautiful wing! It looks like a lace tablecloth."

When everyone gathered around to look, Miss Mackle said, "You can each take a turn during activity time."

"But I want to see the lacy wing

now! I never get a chance to do anything," Mary complained. Then she yawned.

Miss Mackle looked at Mary. "Are you getting enough sleep? You seem out of sorts."

Mary rubbed her eyes. "Grandma thinks I'm in bed sleeping, but I'm really watching TV from the top of the stairs. When mom and dad get home from that *dumb* class, I sneak back into bed."

Miss Mackle raised her eyebrows. "I hope you're getting enough sleep. It's very important."

Later that morning when the teacher was reading aloud, Mary just doodled. Each time she drew a black dog, she slashed a big red X through it.

"So, class," Miss Mackle said closing her book, "do you think Ramona was a pest?"

Mary looked up from her doodling. "I think Ramona was a big *fat* pest. She pulled Susan's hair, she made silly noises during naptime, and she tried to kiss Davey. Everyone knows you're not supposed to kiss boys in school."

Harry shrugged. "I wouldn't mind if she kissed me."

"Aaauuuugh," we gagged.

Song Lee giggled and snorted. When everyone finally calmed down, Miss Mackle continued, "So, Song Lee, what do you think?"

Song Lee beamed. "Ramona isn't a pest."

Mary sat up and shot a look at Song Lee. She did not like it when anyone disagreed with her.

"She loved Susan's corkscrew curls," Song Lee said. "She liked to *boing*

them. She didn't mean to be silly during naptime. She was just pretending to be asleep. I do that too. See?"

Song Lee dropped her head, closed her eyes, and made two very loud snores, "HON *shoooo!* HON *shoooo!*"

Everyone laughed but Mary. She was too busy biting and chewing on her braid. Her rotten mood was as mean and angry as the dark clouds gathering outside our classroom window.

I could tell something bad was going to happen.

I *hoped* it was just a storm.

Garbage Can Kickball

By one o'clock, lightning forks lit up the dark sky. Seconds later, we heard a loud crack of thunder! Miss Mackle walked over to the window. "Does anyone have an idea what we can do for recess?"

Harry flashed his white teeth. "Go outside?"

Song Lee was the only one who laughed.

"Well," I suggested, "we could play seven-up, or four corners."

"Or doggie, doggie who has the bone?" Sidney added.

"I'm not playing any *doggie* game!" Mary protested.

"Okay," I said. "How about kickball in the gym?"

"I hate kickball," Sidney complained. "I always make an out."

Song Lee raised her hand. "We could play *garbage can* kickball."

"Garbage can what?" Dexter asked.

"Garbage can kickball," Song Lee repeated.

"Cool," Harry replied. "I like kicking cans."

Song Lee snickered. "You don't kick

cans. You kick a kickball and try to run home before the pitcher gets it into the garbage can."

"Kind of like kickball," Dexter said.

"Except there is no foul ball, and you have to get a homer each time," Song Lee explained. "Most people make outs."

"*All right!*" Sidney cheered.

After we shot Sid a silent look, Miss Mackle took a class vote. It was unanimous. We all went downstairs in the gym to play garbage can kickball.

Miss Mackle divided us into two teams and then set a wastepaper basket on the pitcher's mound.

"I'm pitcher!" Harry announced as he grabbed the ball.

Mary weaseled her way to the front

13

of the kicking line. "I'm up first," she said in a bossy voice.

Harry rolled a fast, bumpy ball over the plate. Mary ran up and kicked it hard. The ball hit the gym wall and bounced back. Harry grabbed it and dropped it into the garbage can.

Plunk!

"*One away,*" Harry yelled.

Mary stopped running. Then she stomped to the end of the kicking line. "I never get to do anything," she mumbled.

When Song Lee got up, it was already two away.

Harry rolled the ball slow and

smooth and over the plate. Song Lee ran up and kicked it with the side of her foot.

"*Go Song Lee!*" Ida yelled.

Song Lee took off! The lights on her sneakers flashed red and blue as she rounded first.

When she touched third, Dexter fished the ball out from under a scoring table. "I forgot there was no foul ball in this game," he grumbled. "You can kick it anywhere in the gym."

Just as Dexter threw it to Harry, Song Lee slid into home plate.

"Safe!" Miss Mackle called, moving her hands to either side.

Everyone slapped Song Lee ten for her home run except Mary. She was pea-green jealous.

When Mary was up again, she

16

kicked the ball to the left like Song
Lee. She rounded first and was on her
way to second. Dexter, who was playing near the scoring table now, fielded
the ball and tossed it to me at short-
stop. I hurled it to Harry.

Harry was about to drop the ball in

the garbage can, when Mary slipped on a plastic baggy someone had dropped from lunch!

Mary went flying across the gym floor. Right on her rear end.

"Are you okay?" Miss Mackle asked.

As soon as Mary nodded yes, Sidney blurted out, "She landed on her *derry air*—that's French for 'buns.'"

Song Lee turned around and covered her mouth. She was giggling.

Mary's eyes bulged out of her sockets. "Song Lee Park! Don't you know it's mean to laugh at someone when they fall?"

Song Lee slowly turned around. "I . . . didn't mean to giggle. It just came out. I'm sorry."

Mary made a monster face. "Oooooh you!" she growled.

We won the garbage can kickball game 3-2 that day, but it was not the beginning of a sweet victory. It was the beginning of a horrible *war.*

The First
"I Hate You" Note

When we got back to class the first bomb landed.

Actually, it was a pink note folded into eighths, sitting like a place card on Song Lee's desk.

Song Lee unfolded it and read it.

Harry and I watched her crumple it up, walk over to the wastepaper basket, and drop it in. When Song Lee took out

20

her cherry blossom handkerchief, and wiped her eyes with it, we knew the note was deadly. Harry and I dashed over to investigate.

It was easy to spot the pink paper, but when I pulled it out of the can, there was something heavy stuck to it.

Sidney's gooey wad of gum.

"Gross!" I said. "Harry, get it off."

Harry flicked it away with two fingers. Stuff like that never bothers him.

We carried the pink note to the one private corner in the room, under the arts and crafts table, and read it aloud.

Harry and I stared at the rebus.

Who would write such a horrible note to the nicest person in our class?

Harry and I ripped up the note into tiny pieces and dropped it like pink confetti into the wastepaper basket.

During math, Harry and I talked. "Do you think Sid the Squid did it?" Harry asked.

"No," I said. "He never remembers to use apostrophes. Besides, he would have added a French word. He's into that now."

Harry nodded. Then we looked over at the teacher. She was writing a number on the blackboard.

"How many blocks does it take to make twenty-three?" Miss Mackle asked.

Mary answered right away. "Five blocks. Two ten sticks and three ones."

"Good."

Mary beamed. She loved being right.

"Can you make the number twenty-three another way?" Miss Mackle asked.

Mary raised her hand again. "We can make twenty-three with fourteen blocks. One ten stick and thirteen ones."

"Good!" Miss Mackle replied. "Is there still another way?"

Harry put a ten stick in each one of his nostrils and stacked three ones in his hand. "Hey, Song Lee!" he whispered. "This is another way."

When Song Lee looked over and didn't giggle, I knew that note *really* bothered her. Song Lee always giggles when Harry is gross, even when she's sad.

After Dexter stacked 23 one blocks in a row, Miss Mackle asked, "Can anyone guess the pattern for these numbers, five, fourteen, and twenty-three? If you think you know, come up and whisper it in my ear."

24

Mary popped out of her seat and whispered something first. Miss Mackle shook her head. "Nice try, Mary."

When Song Lee whispered something, Miss Mackle threw her arms in the air. "You got it!" Miss Mackle announced.

Song Lee hardly smiled.

Mary tugged on her sweater as she passed by her desk. "You can tell me the math secret," she whispered. "I'm your friend."

When Song Lee shook her head, Mary gritted her teeth. "That's it!" she snarled. "I've had it!"

Oh no, I thought. What was Mary going to do now?

The Rebus Is Solved!

Ten minutes later I found out.

We were putting away our math blocks when the second mysterious note popped up on Song Lee's desk.

Harry and I watched Song Lee read it, rip it in two, and drop it into the garbage.

As soon as she returned to her seat, we raced over and fished out both pink

papers, then fit them together like two
puzzle pieces.

Harry clenched his fist. "How could someone talk like that to Song Lee!"

I looked at the signature. "If we solve that rebus, we'll know who it is."

"Yeah," Harry said leaning over my shoulder. "So what's the drawing? Smoke?"

"There's no N in smoke. It has to be a picture of something with N in it," I said. "What about string?"

I rewrote the letters. "That would spell *strig*. Or maybe *girts*."

"Snake?" Harry suggested.

"Nah," I said, "it looks too much like a ball of string. Wait a minute. A ball of . . . *yarn*!"

"*Yarn* minus N is *yar*," Harry said. "Hey, that spells *Ray* backwards!"

Harry and I slapped each other five.

Then we realized there was no Ray in our room.

"Okay, Ray plus M. What's that? It sure doesn't spell X-ray," I joked.

"It isn't funny," Harry scolded. "There's a *pink rat* in this room and we have to find out who he is. *Mayr?*"

Suddenly, I snapped my fingers. "How dumb can we be!" I said. "It's not a *he*. It's a she! *Song Lee's so-called friend!*"

We turned and looked at Mary.

She was yawning again as she cleaned her glasses with a piece of *pink* paper.

Harry clenched the pink papers in his fist and threw them in the garbage.

"Mary," he grumbled.

"Yeah," I said.

"So what do we do?" I asked. "Tell the teacher?"

"No way!" Harry refused. "I've never tattled in my life. I don't rat on people."

When we looked over at Song Lee, she had her head down on her desk.

"I bet she asks to go home," I moaned.

"Yeah," Harry agreed.

Then he looked me square in the eye. "I'm doing it!"

"What?" I asked.

"You'll see."

Harry Tattles!

This was a first.

There I sat, watching history in the making.

Harry tiptoed up to the teacher and tattled.

I watched Miss Mackle's mouth drop. Then her eyebrows went up and down like an elevator. "Thank you, Harry," she said in a stern voice.

After Harry returned, I looked him square in the eye. "I thought you said you never tattled on people?"

Harry grinned. "I don't. Just on pink rats."

I slapped my buddy five. "Good going."

Harry held up a fist and pumped it in the air. "I can't wait to see Mary get punished."

"Me either," I said.

We watched the teacher walk over to the wastepaper basket, pick out the two halves of the pink note and match them together. As she read the message, Harry rubbed his hands together.

"Boy, is Mary going to get it now!" he said.

"Wait a minute," I said, "where's the teacher going?"

"She's . . . looking for something on our bookshelf," Harry groaned. He leaned forward and rested his chin on his hand. "She's not bawling out Mary. That's for sure!"

"Boys and girls," Miss Mackle called. "Please come over to the library corner and sit down. I have a special story to read."

Story? We already had one today about Ramona.

Reluctantly, we joined the class on the rug. Song Lee was the last one to sit down. I noticed she slouched.

"Life's not fair," Harry mumbled.

"Yeah," I agreed.

Neither of us were prepared for what was about to happen next.

The Dead Flies

When Miss Mackle opened up a picture book by Bernard Waber, Harry shook his head.

She was reading *Lovable Lyle*.

I rolled my eyes. Some punishment, I thought.

But when the teacher got to the middle of the story, I began nodding my head.

Lyle was getting "I hate you" notes from someone in the neighborhood.

"Look," I whispered to Harry. "The pink rat is starting to squirm."

Song Lee sat up and listened.

When Miss Mackle finished, she asked, "What do you think about Clover Sue Hipple?"

I shot my hand in the air.

"Doug?"

"She was mean to send Lyle those hate notes. She made Lyle feel bad for a long time. Lyle had lots of friends because he was kind. I would never want to have a friend like Clover Sue Hipple."

"Me either!" Harry blurted out.

Mary closed her eyes, and plugged her ears.

"I bet Clover Sue Hipple wouldn't like it if *she* got an 'I hate you' note," Ida suggested.

"Well," Miss Mackle sighed. "I hope I never see another 'I hate you' note in my class."

We all shook our heads.

Except Mary. Her eyes were still closed and her ears were still plugged.

Suddenly, Sidney looked at the clock and shouted, *"Activity time!"* He darted over to the microscope to observe the fly.

There was a long line at the science table, so Harry and I went to a computer and turned on the Oregon Trail. That's a neat program on our hard drive. You get to pretend you're on a wagon going West.

"Let's include Mary in our camp," I said. "Maybe she'll get bitten by a snake."

Harry smiled as he typed Mary's name in our group—with his, mine, and Song Lee's. Our wagon was ready to roll West for new adventures on the screen!

When I looked to see what Song Lee was doing, I noticed she was under the arts and crafts table making something.

I sighed, "I guess Song Lee has forgotten how mean Mary has been to her. Song Lee is just too nice."

While Harry and I were at the computer, Mary took a turn at the microscope. Then she yawned as she looked around for the jar of flies. "What did you do with the rest of them Sidney? I wanted to make another slide."

Sidney shrugged. *"Junn say pa—*that's French for 'I don't know.'"

"You . . ." Mary groaned, *"fair may la bush!"*

"It's *la boosh,*" Sidney said, puckering his lips.

Mary stomped off. She hated being corrected.

At that moment, Song Lee came

over and joined us at the computer table. "How's it going?" she asked.

"Well," Harry said, "Doug and I are doing great, but you have a broken leg, and Mary has dysentery."

We knew what *that* meant. We had looked it up in the dictionary the first day we played the Oregon Trail. Dysentery meant you had the runs.

When Song Lee and I cracked up, I knew she was feeling better about things.

Then Mary appeared. "What's so funny?" she demanded.

"Nothing," we fibbed.

"Did you see the jar of flies?"

"I did," Song Lee said. "It's over there."

Mary abruptly turned to where

Song Lee was pointing. There on her desk was an empty peanut butter jar. Beside it was . . .

. . . a pink note.

A pink note folded in half, sitting like a giant place card. It looked just like the ones Song Lee had gotten except it was much bigger, and it had Mary's name on it!

Mary slowly made her way toward the note, tiptoeing between the desks as if there were land mines.

Harry and I watched from behind the computer.

As soon as Mary got to her desk, she picked up the pink note and opened it.

"AAAAAUUUUGH!" she screamed.

"Ohhh!" I groaned. "I wish I knew what that note said."

Song Lee cupped her hand and giggled, "It says . . .

Dear Mary,
Don't send any more 'I hate you' notes.
It's mean.
Signed,

The dead flies."

Harry and I did a double take.
"Man, *you* made that deadly note?"
I asked.
Song Lee nodded. "I glued the flies
right on the paper. Neat-o huh?"
Harry pumped his fist while I rolled
my eyes.
Miss Mackle rushed over to Mary.
"That was some bloodcurdling cry. Are
you okay?"

47

The class gathered around Mary.

"I'm okay," Mary groaned. "Someone put this pink note on my desk. See? Isn't that the meanest thing! There are dead flies glued right on it! It's gross!"

Miss Mackle shrugged. "Why would someone tell *you* not to write 'I hate you' notes?"

Mary gulped some air before she answered. Then she looked over at Song Lee, who was peeking from behind the computer. "I ... I ..." she gasped. "I ... may ... have," Mary's voice got lower and lower. "... have sent one to ... someone ... once or twice."

"Ohhh." Miss Mackle nodded. "So that's what this is all about."

Mary's eyes suddenly got all watery.

She turned and walked over to Song Lee.

48

Harry and I watched.

So did the class.

When Song Lee stepped out from behind the computer, the girls were face to face.

It kind of reminded me of an old western movie. All they had to do was

put up their dukes and punch each other out.

"Did you do this?" Mary demanded. She held up the pink note and crunched it.

Song Lee answered, "Yes. I wanted to show you what it feels like to get a mean note."

Mary paused as she wiped away some tears with the sleeve of her sweater. "You really . . . *bugged* me back."

"Look," Harry said. "Mary is crying and laughing at the same time."

"Yeah," I said, "and now they're hugging each other."

I could tell Mary was sorry. She even started coming to school in a better mood. I bet she was going to bed on time.

And she never sent another "I hate you" note again. Thanks to Song Lee and her dead flies.

I think Mary learned that if you do mean things, they *can* come back to bug you.